For Henry Hardy — AF

For my Frome Brownies — EF

STRIPES PUBLISHING
An imprint of Little Tiger Press
1 The Coda Centre, 189 Munster Road,
London SW6 6AW

A paperback original
First published in Great Britain in 2016

Text copyright © Adam Frost, 2016
Illustrations copyright © Emily Fox, 2016
Back cover images courtesy of www.shutterstock.com

ISBN: 978-1-84715-665-5

A CIP catalogue record for this book is available
from the British Library.

Printed and bound in the UK.

10 9 8 7 6 5 4 3 2 1

Fox Investigates

A Web of Lies

ADAM FROST

ILLUSTRATED BY EMILY FOX

DOUBLE TROUBLE

It was a fine spring morning when Wily Fox walked out of New York's JFK airport and got into a yellow taxicab.

"The Sheep residence, please," he said to the driver.

"You sure about that, buddy?" the taxi driver replied. "You know the old lady's a recluse. She don't open her door to nobody."

Wily smiled. "It's OK. I've got someone on the inside."

The taxi driver shrugged and drove off. After a few minutes he glanced up at his rear-view mirror.

"Hey, I know you," he said.

Wily grew tense. He didn't like being recognized. As the world's greatest detective, it was his job to stay in the shadows.

"Yeah, you're that Fox guy. I've seen your picture in the papers."

Wily thought about his recent cases. The fiendish forger and the perfume plot. Would they have been in the US press? There was that time when the president had lost her address book containing the names of every single American spy and Wily had helped her to find it. (It had been wedged under her desk to stop it wobbling.) But that had been top secret.

"Yeah," the taxi driver went on, "you're that singer, Finlay Fox. Go on, give us a tune."

Wily relaxed. "Sorry, that's not me, I'm afraid."

"Really?" said the taxi driver. "Well, you look just like him. He's like your double. Or you're his double."

Wily smiled. He didn't believe in doubles. Everyone was unique – if you knew what to look for.

Wily rapped hard on the large oak door of the Sheep residence. The building itself was old and grand, but it was gloomy, with cracked windows and ivy creeping up every wall. The young sheep who answered the door started talking before Wily even had a chance to introduce himself.

"I don't know how he's done it. He's the double of my brother!" she blurted out.

"What? Who's a double?" said Wily, confused.

"Sorry – where are my manners," said the sheep. "Come inside, and I'll tell you everything."

Wily followed the sheep through a huge entrance hall, down a long corridor and into an enormous sitting room. There were cracks in the ceiling and the furniture looked old and threadbare.

The sheep offered Wily a faded armchair.

"I'll start from the beginning," she said, sitting down opposite him. "First of all, I'm Sally Sheep. I take it you received my email."

"Yes, I came right away. It sounded urgent," said Wily.

"It *is* urgent," said Sally. "My grandmother – Sheila Sheep – is one of the wealthiest animals in America. My parents died when I was young and she brought me up, along with my twin brother, Simon."

Wily nodded. "I've done my homework."

"Of course," said Sally. "So you'll also know that two years ago, my brother left home to go on a scientific trip to Peru. He went to the Amazon to study the nine-legged tree spider, one of the rarest creatures in the world. But here's something you won't know. Two months ago, we lost all contact with him.

There were no phone calls, no emails, nothing. For the first few weeks, we assumed he was ill and that's why he couldn't write. Another month passed, and we started to panic. We were about to contact the US embassy in Peru when…"

"He called you?" asked Wily.

"He came back," said Sally. "Only it's not him. It's an impostor."

"Right," said Wily. "Then why did you let him in?"

"I didn't," said Sally. "The butler did. And he took him straight to my grandmother's room. She's very old. Very sick. She hasn't been outside for more than a decade. And she always *adored* Simon. So she *wants* to believe it's him. It looks just like him, but I know it isn't."

"What makes you so sure?" asked Wily.

"He's my twin," said Sally. "We've always been able to read each other's minds.

But from this animal I get … nothing. That's why I called you! I don't want to confront him until we know what he's done with my brother."

"But this sheep looks like Simon?" said Wily.

"That's the thing," said Sally. "He's the spitting image. He's even wearing the watch that my grandmother gave him for his eighteenth birthday."

"Hmm," said Wily, "the two sheep must have met, then. And the impostor must have stolen the watch. And he's presumably come here because he wants your grandmother's money."

"Of course," huffed Sally, "but I don't care about that. All *I* want to know is what he's done with my brother. He's alive – I can sense it! Find him, Mr Fox, before it's too late."

"OK. Describe Simon to me. What are his distinguishing features?" said Wily.

"He has a black patch of wool on his ear,"

said Sally. "He's allergic to nuts and he has a zig-zag scar on his left hand."

"That's a good start," said Wily. "And now I should meet this impostor. Is he here?"

Sally shook her head. "He's out shopping, spending money with my grandmother's credit cards, no doubt. But it's the Millionaire's Ball tonight. He'll be there, along with all the richest animals in New York."

"Can you get me an invite?" asked Wily.

Sally nodded. "You can be my guest. Meet me in the lobby of the Empire State Building at eight p.m. sharp."

"I'll be there," said Wily. As he stood up, he added, "Mind if I have a look around on my way out?"

"Go ahead," said Sally, "but don't go near my grandmother's room. She can't find out that I've hired you."

Wily thanked her and walked back towards the huge entrance hall. He glanced up the large staircase and saw a row of bedroom doors. He climbed the stairs.

The first room he went in belonged to Sally. Wily glanced around and immediately noticed an unusual statue on her bedside table. It was a carved wooden monkey grinning from ear to ear. On the bottom was engraved:

TO MY DEAR SISTER,
A GIFT FROM THE AMAZON
LOVE, SIMON X

Wily put the statue down, but then he saw something glinting in the monkey's eye. He tugged it with his finger and a tiny microphone attached to a wire came out.

Looks like this monkey has bugs, Wily thought. *Now why would Simon want to listen in on his sister's conversations?*

He put the microphone in his pocket, glanced around the room again and left.

Wily quickly searched the other rooms on the landing – two bathrooms, a guest bedroom and a small study – then he found what looked like Simon's room.

It was very tidy. A row of clean suits in the wardrobe, neatly folded shirts in the drawers. In the bedside table, Wily found Simon's passport. Wily checked the watermark on the back cover. It was genuine. This meant one of two things: that the real

NAME **SIMON SHEEP**
PLACE OF BIRTH **NEW YORK USA**
DATE OF BIRTH **01/04/1995**

Simon had returned and Sally was wrong. Or that his passport had been stolen from the real Simon, along with the watch.

Wily looked at the mirror on the wall above Simon's bed. He stared at his reflection and thought about the case.

Let's assume that Sally is right and that Simon is a crook, Wily said to himself. *He's conjured up a plan to get Sheila Sheep's money. That explains why, but it doesn't explain how. How has the fake Simon managed to make himself look exactly like the real Simon, so that passport officials and even his own grandmother think he's the real thing?*

Wily took a step closer. The mirror suddenly shattered with an ear-splitting crash. Glass splinters exploded across the room. Wily ducked and spun round as he heard the door shut.

He dashed out on to the landing, but no one was there. He ran back into the room and looked at the space where the mirror had been. A poison dart was lodged in the wall and green liquid dripped from its tip.

Wily grabbed the dart and carefully pulled it out.

"Another gift from the Amazon," he growled. "I wonder what Albert will make of this."

FRIENDS IN HIGH PLACES

Albert Mole worked behind the scenes, helping Wily on all his cases. Whenever the detective needed a gadget or information, Albert was ready with it. This time Albert had set up their temporary headquarters in the Statue of Liberty's torch. Right now he was sitting behind a desk, surrounded by computer screens, staring at the poison dart.

"And you didn't see who fired this?" he asked.

Wily shook his head. "They left nothing. No footprints, no fingerprints."

"Well, it's poison all right," said Albert. "From the purple-bottomed tree frog. You only get them in a very small area of the Amazon."

"No one else knows I'm here," said Wily, "which suggests Simon is a fake. The real Simon had no reason to kill me and then run away."

"True," said Albert. "We need to take a closer look at him. Give me your phone." Wily handed it over. "I'm transferring the latest face-mapping app on to your hard drive," Albert explained. "And a DNA analyzer. Remember how to use them?"

Wily nodded.

"There – you're good to go," said Albert.

Wily arrived at the Empire State Building dressed in his smartest suit. He could see Sally waiting in the lobby. She was wearing a bright red dress and extremely high heels.

"Are you ready?" she asked.

Wily nodded. They stepped into a lift and Sally pushed the button for the top floor.

"What's the plan?" she asked, as they rocketed upwards.

Wily took out his phone.

"You're going to phone for help?" Sally asked, raising an eyebrow.

"I've got a photo of your brother on here," said Wily. "And tonight I'm going to take a photo of the impostor and run it against face-mapping technology. Find out if he's the real deal."

"He isn't. I've told you," Sally protested.

"We still need to prove it," said Wily. "I also need this. Excuse me."

He leaned forwards, grabbed a strand of wool from Sally's neck and pulled it out with a...

DOINGGG!!

"Er ... ow?" said Sally, looking confused.

Wily pushed it against the screen of his phone until he heard a beep.

"As you're his twin," he explained, "your wool will be very similar to Simon's. I just need to get some of his wool to compare it with."

The lift doors opened and Wily and Sally stepped out into a large ballroom. Wily was nearly blinded by the bright lights and shiny jewellery.

Then a big woolly face appeared in front of them. "My darling sister!" it grinned. "I didn't realize you were coming! Who's your charming companion?"

"Hello, Simon. This is Wily."

Wily couldn't believe his eyes – the sheep really was the spitting image of Simon. Wily was expecting a good disguise, but this was uncanny. The eyes, the ears, the soft fleece, the scar on his hand – the impostor had *become* Simon.

Wily had to think fast. "Pleased to meet you," he said. "Mind if I take a photo of you and your beautiful sister?"

"Go ahead," said Simon. He put his arm round Sally as the detective snapped away. Then Wily pressed a button and a green bar passed across the screen of his phone. The name "Simon Sheep" appeared.

The faces were an exact match.

"Now, if you'll excuse me, I must mingle," said Simon. "I haven't seen most of these animals since I got back from Peru."

"Hang on, we've got a bit tangled," said Wily. The button on his sleeve had got caught up with the wool on Simon's arm.

"Don't worry, always happening. Time I had a shear," said Simon with a smile. He pulled his arm free and sauntered off.

Wily looked down and removed the coil of wool from under his button. He held the wool against his phone screen until he heard a beep. A message appeared:

SAMPLE MATCH.
RELATIONSHIP:
BROTHER AND
SISTER.

Wily turned to Sally, who was staring furiously at her brother as he drifted round the room, chatting to everyone.

"I don't understand it," said Wily. "The DNA scan says it's really him."

"B-but, it isn't … it isn't," stammered Sally.

"I believe you," Wily said, "but *how* has he managed it? That's the fascinating question. Don't worry – I'll find the answer."

Wily watched Simon for the rest of the evening, as the sheep chatted and danced and ate. Simon talked about his trip to the Amazon and the spiders he had been studying. He didn't do or say anything suspicious.

Wily moved on to the balcony to consider his next move. He could see Simon drinking orange juice and eating a sandwich.

"Peanut butter! My favourite!" he heard the sheep exclaim.

Wily looked down at the city far below. There were skyscrapers on all sides and, in the distance, the sea. Had the investigation reached a dead end? He needed to prove that Simon wasn't Simon, but so far he couldn't.

However he knew one thing for certain. Animals with nothing to hide don't try to kill you. And Simon – or someone close to him – had tried to shoot Wily with a poisoned dart.

Then Wily's eyebrows shot up with delight. "Peanut butter!" he cried out.

He was about to turn round, when he felt a pair of strong hands on his back.

They pushed him off the balcony and down he fell.

KING OF THE SWINGERS

As Wily plummeted from the top of the Empire State Building, he had time to reflect. Literally. In the windows of the skyscraper, he could see the reflection of a fox. A fox that looked shocked and scared.

Come on, Wily, he said to himself, *you need to save yourself. THINK!*

As he tumbled, every few milliseconds, his reflection vanished. Instead, he'd get a glimpse of desks and chairs. Which could mean only one thing – some of the windows were open.

That gave Wily an idea. The next time his reflection vanished, he stuck out his arm. His paw found a ledge, but it slipped out of his grasp.

A split second later, he tried again – and missed again.

The ground was getting closer and closer. Wily had one more chance. Maybe.

Windows and reflections … windows and reflections. Suddenly there was a gap. Wily did a kung-fu kick – as he stuck out his leg, his foot got tangled in an office blind. He was jerked upside down and left dangling ten floors up, staring at the ground below. Then Wily heard the blind crinkle and give way.

27

He quickly flipped himself up, scrambled up the blind and hopped on to the window ledge.

Wily found himself in an office bathroom. Opposite him was a sink and a mirror. In the mirror he could see his reflection again. Only this time it was grinning.

Half an hour later, Wily was sitting in Albert's HQ. He was still feeling a bit shaky after his near-death experience. He was staring at one of Albert's computer screens, on a video call with a very cross sheep.

"Where did you go?" asked Sally. "I'm that close to giving you the push."

"I think your so-called brother already did that," said Wily. He quickly explained what had happened. "It was either him or someone working for him," he said. "Though I can't prove that right now. And I can't prove he's not Simon, either."

"I promise you he isn't..." said Sally.

"I *know* he isn't," said Wily. "You said he had a nut allergy."

"He does. We both do," said Sally.

"Well, I saw Simon eating a peanut butter sandwich earlier. He even said it was his favourite. The impostor has changed his outside, but he hasn't changed his *inside*."

"So that *does* prove it!" Sally exclaimed, looking excited.

"It's not enough by itself. We need more evidence. I've got to find your brother."

"But ... but ... he could be anywhere. Where are you going to start?"

"Peru," said Wily. "Where he was seen last. And as the fake Simon stole his passport,

I suspect he's still there."

"But that could take forever. Can't you force this impostor to talk? Make him tell you where Simon is? They could be starving him, torturing him…"

Wily shook his head. "If the impostor thinks we're on to him, then he can just make one phone call and your brother is…" Wily trailed off, not wanting to scare Sally. "We have to tread carefully," he finished.

"This is terrible," Sally said. "If we act too quickly, they may kill him. But if we act too slowly, he may die."

"The fake Simon won't kill your brother unless he has to," said Wily. "But you're right – we have to act fast. Your brother is in the hands of a ruthless villain. So I must leave straight away."

"OK," said Sally.

"There's just one thing I need you to do," Wily said.

"Name it," said Sally.

"Ask the fake Simon if he's seen the fox you went to the ball with. Tell him I've vanished without trace. That way, the impostor will think he's killed me. And he won't follow me to Peru."

"OK."

"And from now on, don't try to contact me. I found a bug in your room earlier…"

"W-what?" Sally stammered, looking around. "Does that mean he can hear—"

"Don't worry," said Wily. "I dealt with it. But he might plant others, so be careful what you say."

Sally nodded. She said goodbye to Wily and then ended the call.

The detective turned to Albert. "So, it looks like we're off to the Amazon," he said.

"What have you got for me?"

"Funny you should ask..." said Albert, and rummaged around in a drawer.

He pulled out a stick.

"You want to play fetch?" asked Wily.

"Point it over there," said Albert, "and press the button at the end."

Wily took the stick. "It's like the baton in a relay race," he said, pushing a small black button with his thumb.

A green ribbon shot out of the end of the stick and glued itself to the far wall. Wily tugged, but it didn't budge.

Wily pushed the button. The ribbon fluttered back inside the stick.

Albert handed Wily a second baton. "You have two sky sticks," he explained.

"Like Spider-Man!" Wily exclaimed. "I could have done with these half an hour ago, when

I was falling off a skyscraper."

"They should help you navigate the jungle," Albert continued. "Aim them at high branches and swing through the canopy."

"Perfect," said Wily. "How do I get there?"

"There's a plane leaving for Iquitos in half an hour," said Albert, "but you'll never make it in time. The next one's in two days."

"TWO DAYS!" said Wily. "I've got to find Simon *now*. I bet I can catch that plane if I use these." He held up the sticks.

"Hang on…" stammered Albert.

"Of course I'll hang on," Wily said, smiling. "That's how they work, isn't it?"

"No, no," grumbled Albert. "I mean, remember what you told Sally. You're supposed to be dead."

"It's late at night," said Wily. "And I'll hide my face."

Albert could see that Wily was determined.

"OK," he said. "But I'd better come with you. You'll need a base in Peru."

Albert quickly packed away his computers and gadgets – they all folded up or telescoped down into a medium-sized suitcase. Then they opened a hatch in the ceiling and climbed out. They were balanced on top of the Statue of Liberty's torch.

"The range is only about two-hundred metres," said Albert. "We'll never make it across the water."

"Don't worry," said Wily. "I've got an idea." He pulled up his coat collar to cover his face. "Jump on," he said.

"I've got a funny feeling I'm going to hate this," Albert said. He clambered on to Wily's back, clutching his suitcase.

"Here we go…" said Wily, then jumped off the Statue of Liberty. They hurtled towards the ground. Halfway down, Wily shot his sky stick back at the torch. The ribbon stuck fast and swung them outwards. Then Wily shot the second stick and retracted the first one at the same time, and they swung further out. By the third swing, they were whirling round at top speed, like they were on a swing-chair ride. Finally, when they were facing the city, he released the sky sticks and they were flung forwards at top speed, as if they'd been shot out of a cannon.

As they cleared the shore and flew towards the skyscrapers, Wily aimed one of the sky sticks at the top-floor windows and fired. It hit its target and they swung forwards. Wily aimed the second sky stick at another skyscraper. The ribbon flew out and they swung forwards again.

"This is working just fine, Albert," said Wily. "Now, which way is the airport?"

But Albert had gone a funny colour and was murmuring something about multi-coloured elephants.

"Don't worry, I'll follow the signs," said Wily.

Wily veered right and headed for Brooklyn Bridge. Occasionally he would hear someone yell something from the ground, but most of the time he was either too high or too fast – and he passed through the city undetected.

Albert stirred as they swung along the top of Brooklyn Bridge. "The plane leaves in twenty minutes," he murmured.

Wily sped up, firing the ribbons further, swinging even faster.

Then Albert mumbled, "My hands have gone numb, Wily. I can't hang on."

"You'll be fine!" replied Wily.

But when he glanced round, Wily saw that Albert was gone. The mole was tumbling towards the ground.

Quick as a flash, Wily shot his second sky stick at Albert. It glued itself to Albert's bottom. Then Wily pressed retract. The stick made a groaning sound as it struggled to haul Albert up. When Albert was close enough, Wily scooped him up and plonked him on his back, just as they swung into the airport car park.

"Is that what they call a sticky end?" said Wily, as he dropped to the ground.

"Very funny," replied Albert, yanking the end of the ribbon from his bottom. "But you got us here in time. Now, let's go and find our plane."

THE GHOST VILLAGE

Five hours later Wily and Albert arrived in Peru.

"Simon was based in a town called Pebas," said Wily, as they walked past the luggage carousel. "That's about a hundred miles away."

"Then we should be there before lunchtime," said Albert.

They walked into the arrivals area and stopped dead. There were about fifty tour guides and taxi drivers waiting for animals to arrive, all holding pieces of card in their hand. Each card had the name of the animal they

were waiting for written on it. Nothing unusual
there. Except they all had the same name.

WILY FOX

"Keep walking," whispered Wily.

Albert nodded and shuffled forwards.

The tour guides and taxi drivers stared at
Wily as he strode past, their heads turning
slowly, their faces showing no emotion.

When they were outside the airport, Albert said, "The fake Simon must know you're still on the case. I *told* you not to swing through the middle of New York."

"I'm not sure it's his style," said Wily. "It feels more like the work of—"

"The police?" said a voice behind them.

"Sybil!" exclaimed Wily and Albert.

It was Sergeant Sybil Squirrel, an officer with PSSST – the Police Spy, Sleuth and Snoop Taskforce. She was sitting on a motorbike with a sidecar.

"It was Julius's idea," said Sybil. "He thought it might scare you off. I knew it wouldn't. That's why I decided to wait here."

Julius was Sybil's boss – a short, angry bulldog who didn't like Wily very much. Mostly because Wily solved a lot more cases than he did.

"But what are PSSST doing in Peru?"
asked Wily.

"We're tracking down a goat called Maxwell
Mirage," said Sybil. "He's a con artist. We've
been on his trail for months. And it's led us
here."

"So where's Julius now?" asked Wily.

"He's on his way with a fleet of police cars.
A PSSST agent spotted you getting on that
plane in New York. Julius thinks you're here
to meddle with his case and he's determined
to stop you. So I've brought you a present,"
said Sybil. She climbed off the motorbike and
gestured towards it.

"Sybil," Wily said, smiling, "you're too good
to us."

"Well, you've saved my life once or twice,"
she said. "But listen, I need your help in
return. I don't know why you're here and

I know you won't tell me. But if you see *any* sign of Maxwell Mirage, phone me. Straight away. Here's a copy of the case files. Now get out of here, quick," she said.

Wily leaped on to the motorbike and Albert jumped into the sidecar. They could see two police cars rounding the corner in front of the airport.

"Thanks, Sybil," shouted Wily.

They watched the police cars in the rear-view mirror as they sped off.

"I don't think they'll catch up with us," said Albert, "but I hope we haven't got Sybil into trouble."

"No way," said Wily. "She's too smart for that. Now, what's in that case file?"

Albert started to skim-read. "Maxwell Mirage," he said, "twenty-five-year-old goat. Nationality British. Master of disguise. Tricked a Brazilian millionaire out of all of her savings by pretending to be her long-lost grandson. Wily ... this is identical to our case."

"Not quite," said Wily. "Simon is definitely a sheep. We sampled his wool, remember? Perhaps the two animals work together?"

"Maybe Maxwell pushed you off the Empire State Building," said Albert, "while the fake Simon was inside."

"What else does it say?" asked Wily.

"Maxwell was caught by Brazilian police trying to leave the country three months ago," said Albert, "but he escaped. They think he fled into the jungle and came to Peru."

"Sounds like another good reason for us to go into the jungle, then," said Wily, nodding at a row of trees on the horizon.

"Pebas is due east," said Albert. "Take the left fork here."

A couple of hours later, they arrived in Pebas's main square. Pebas was a small town on the banks of the Amazon. It was full of shops and restaurants. The streets were covered with decorations, streamers and flower garlands from a recent fiesta. There was only one thing wrong. The town was empty.

"What do you think happened?" asked Albert. "Looks like they were throwing a party."

"Let's find out," said Wily, getting off the motorbike. "You look for clues along here. I'll explore the side streets."

As Wily moved away from the main square, the roads became tracks and there were more trees than houses. He got out his sky sticks.

"Time for a proper look around," he murmured.

He shot a ribbon towards a nearby tree and swung through the town.

Tucked in among the trees, he saw small shacks covered in bunting and tiny huts festooned with flags. All of them were empty.

Why would all these animals leave their homes at once? And could it be connected to Simon Sheep's disappearance?

As Wily swung back towards Albert, he saw another hut in a clearing. This one looked like it had been abandoned long ago, as it was covered in cobwebs. He was about to swing away when a thought popped into his head: *the nine-legged tree spider.* The rarest spider in the world. The spider that Simon had been researching.

In a flash, Wily was in front of the shack,
tugging the cobwebs away from the windows.
A couple of baby tree spiders
scuttled away from his paw.

Inside, Wily could see a
workbench, some empty
boxes and a giant picture of a
spider taped to the far wall. His
heart beat faster. The secret of
Simon's disappearance could be
in this shack. He was about to push
the door open when he heard a squeaky voice
behind him.

"Hold it right there, señor," it said.

Wily turned round and saw a guinea pig
holding a catapult.

"You are a horrible bandit," said the guinea
pig. "You might have scared away all my
friends, but you won't scare *me*."

"Hang on a second…" said Wily.

"Any last words before I shoot you?" asked the guinea pig, pulling back his catapult.

"Look, look…" Wily stammered.

The guinea pig pulled the elastic further.

"I'm a friend of Simon's!" Wily protested, just as the guinea pig released the pellet.

BANDIT COUNTRY

At the last moment, as Wily said "Simon", the guinea pig jerked his catapult upwards and shot the pellet at a tree.

"A friend of Simon's!" the guinea pig exclaimed. "Why didn't you say?" He ran forwards and grabbed Wily's hand with both of his paws, shaking it enthusiastically. "My brother!" he declared.

At the same time, four other guinea pigs emerged from the trees. They were camouflaged to blend in with their surroundings, with swipes of brown paint on their faces and twigs and leaves tied to their backs.

"I am Julio," announced the guinea pig with the catapult, "and these are my friends Pepe, Sergio, Pablo and Maria."

The other guinea pigs all came forwards and bowed.

"Pleased to meet you and everything," said Wily, "but where's Simon?"

"Ah, that is a very sad story," said Julio, shaking his head. "It also explains why everyone is hiding in the jungle like frightened mice."

"Is Simon dead?" asked Wily.

Julio glanced at his friends. "We don't know. Simon used to live in this hut, studying our famous nine-legged tree spiders. Anyway, two months ago, the bandits came."

"Where from?" asked Wily.

"Across the mountains," said Julio. "We were halfway through our annual festival when they poured into the main square, shooting their arrows and flashing their knives. They all wore cloaks with big hoods, so I don't know what animals they were, but they were much bigger than us."

"We were all dressed in our carnival outfits," said Pepe.

"What chance did we have?" said Maria.

"So we ran away as fast as we could," said Sergio sadly.

"I raced up here to warn Simon," said Julio, "but he said he wouldn't leave. He hadn't finished his research and what could the bandits do to him? When we came back to explore the town a few days later, his hut was empty and he was gone."

"GONE!" wailed Maria.

"Hang on," said Wily. "There was no dead body?"

Julio shook his head.

"Yet he said he refused to leave," Wily mused.

"That's right," said Julio. "He wouldn't have run away. Not with all his research here."

"This makes no sense," said Wily.

"There's something else," said Julio. "Simon's assistant has vanished, too. Gustavo Goat."

"Gustavo Goat?" said Wily. "His sister didn't say he had an assistant."

"He hadn't been here long," said Julio. "Maybe only a month. But he was as crazy about spiders as Simon was."

"OK," said Wily. "I need to have a look inside that hut. Let's get rid of these cobwebs."

Wily started brushing the cobwebs away from the door and the windows.

"Er, señor, I wouldn't do that if I were you," said Julio.

"It's OK, the spiders can make new webs," said Wily, continuing to brush the sticky strands away.

"It's not that, it's just..."

The house groaned and shivered and then started to slip forwards.

Wily instinctively jumped out of the way.

"The cobwebs are the only thing keeping it in place!" exclaimed Julio.

The hut slid down the hill towards the town. As it went faster and faster, planks of wood started to splinter and fly off the sides. Soon it was just the floorboards, the front of the hut and Simon's workbench hurtling down the hill.

Wily thought fast. Any clues he could hope for would probably be in that workbench.

He shot both his sky sticks at the legs of the bench. They latched on.

The sky sticks went taut and began to drag Wily down the hill after the hut.

"Help me!" he cried.

The guinea pigs grabbed on behind Wily, forming a mini tug-of-war team.

It was just enough to stop the workbench in its tracks.

The rest of the hut crashed into a row of trees and splintered into hundreds of pieces.

"Now that's what I call a mobile home," said Wily. "Thanks for your help, my friends."

He tied the sky sticks to a tree to secure the workbench, and then ran down the hill to examine it. Julio and his friends scampered behind him.

Wily opened the first drawer. There was a pot of strange red seeds.

"Groundfern seeds," said Julio. "The nine-legged tree spider's favourite food. They eat hundreds every day."

He opened the second drawer. A diary.

"Oh, yes," Julio said. "Simon was always scribbling away in that."

The third drawer was deeper than the others. It was also locked. Wily pulled out a pin from his pocket and picked the lock. He opened the drawer slowly, expecting money or a weapon, but there was just a bundle of wool stuffed in it. He felt round the edge of the drawer – no, there was nothing else in there, just the wool.

"Simon's?" asked Wily.

Julio nodded. "He found it very hot out here. He would shear himself every few weeks. I didn't know he kept his old coats though."

"Maybe he didn't," said Wily. He pointed at the front of the drawer. It was labelled "Gustavo's drawer".

"You said Gustavo was a goat?" said Wily.

Julio nodded.

Instantly Wily remembered Maxwell Mirage – the con artist that Sybil and PSSST were

chasing. Were Gustavo and Maxwell the same
goat? And was Maxwell now the fake Simon?
Maxwell had escaped from police custody and
fled into the jungle. Perhaps he'd pretended
to be interested in nine-legged tree spiders
in order to befriend Simon and then steal his
identity?

Wily glanced up at the diary on the
workbench. The answers might be in there.
He turned to the first page, but it was just a
series of strange symbols.

"What language is this?" he asked.

Julio craned his neck forwards. "Ah, that's

Ulbuti, one of the native languages here. Simon was trying to learn it. He practised all the time. Pablo speaks it fluently."

The smallest of the guinea pigs stepped forwards and bowed.

"Señor, it would give me the greatest honour to translate this for you," said Pablo.

Wily handed him the diary.

Pablo cleared his throat. "*I have been in the jungle for two weeks now and I think I have finally gained the trust of the kind-hearted townsfolk* – that's us," he said, smiling proudly.

"Just skip to the parts that mention Gustavo Goat," said Wily.

"OK," said Pablo. "*Very exciting! A new arrival in the village. His name is Gustavo Goat and he also wants to study the spiders. He too admires the speed at which they build their webs. And their incredible waterproof silk.*"

Pablo scanned through the next couple of pages. "Here's the next entry about Gustavo," he said. "*Gustavo and I have argued. He keeps asking me questions about my life back in New York. I keep saying that I don't want to talk about it, I'm not going back until my research is complete. But he keeps asking and asking. Why? My underpants are full of custard…* Ah, he is using an Ulbuti saying there, it means 'I am confused'."

"Any other mentions?" asked Wily.

Pablo skimmed forwards. "Just this one," he said. "This is the day before the bandits came. *Gustavo has gone. I finally gave up and told him a few details about my family. He looked happy at last. But this morning, his hammock was empty. He didn't take any of his own clothes, but one of my suits is missing and he has taken my watch and my passport.*

Even stranger: I sheared my wool yesterday because of the heat and left it underneath my hammock. That's gone, too. What possible use could he have for my old wool?"

Wily's mind was racing. A clear picture was starting to form. Maxwell had become Gustavo and then  Simon. He could have fooled Wily's DNA detector by making a coat out of Simon's sheared wool.

Only three things bothered him.

Firstly: Maxwell may have put on a woolly coat, but how had he managed to fool Simon's grandmother? Goats and sheep looked similar, but not THAT similar.

Secondly: how had Maxwell managed to get out of the country with the whole of PSSST looking for him?

Thirdly and most importantly: what had Maxwell done with Simon?

Wily couldn't go back to New York and confront Maxwell. Not yet. Not without more evidence. He turned to face the guinea pigs.

"I need to find Simon," he said. "Have you *any* idea what happened to him?"

The guinea pigs looked at one another.

"Only the bandits can tell you that," said Maria.

"Then I need to find the bandits," said Wily.

"They will kill you, señor," said Pablo. "Shoot you with their poison arrows."

"Their what?"

"They use poison arrows to defend themselves," said Pablo.

Wily remembered the poison dart that had nearly killed him at the Sheep residence. Were the bandits and Maxwell working together?

"OK, now I really need to find them," said Wily.

"Where's their hideout?"

"Somewhere in the mountains," said Julio. "But they're never in it. They're all on the same ridiculous quest."

"What quest?" asked Wily. "What are you talking about?"

At that point, there was a rustling in the bushes. Julio spun round and aimed his catapult at the noise. A few seconds later, Albert emerged holding a large sheet of paper.

"Wily!" he exclaimed. "Fancy going on a treasure hunt?"

THE TREASURE TRAIL

Albert walked towards Wily, holding what looked like a treasure map in his hands.

"Don't look at it, señor," whispered Maria.

"No good comes to anyone who tries to find the Lost Treasure of Tunza-Dosh," warned Julio. "It's cursed."

"Lost treasure?" said Wily.

"I've read about this," said Albert, "but I thought it was just a legend."

"No, it's real," said Julio. "The treasure is hidden in the jungle. Only fools look for it."

"Fools," said Maria, "and bandits."

"The road to the jungle passes through our town," said Julio. "The bandits stopped to steal our money and possessions. One of them must have dropped that map."

"So that's where they'll be," said Wily. "On the road to Tunza-Dosh. If we find them, we'll find out what happened to Simon."

Albert laid the treasure map on the ground and flattened it out.

"That's the main square," said Julio.

"Are there ferns growing up here?" asked Wily.

"There never used to be," said Julio, "but things change fast in the jungle. Let's go and look."

Wily retrieved his sky sticks – the workbench slid into a ditch with a thud – and followed Julio through the trees.

As they walked, Wily told Albert what he'd discovered in the hut and his theory about Maxwell. A few minutes later, they were standing on the edge of town, looking at a narrow track that led into a dark patch of palm trees.

"There, Wily, there!" cried Albert.

He pointed at a row of ferns that were growing along the side of the track. They appeared at regular two-metre intervals, as if they'd been planted that way deliberately.

"The quest begins!" said Wily, stepping forwards boldly.

But Julio and his fellow guinea pigs didn't move.

"We told you. The treasure is cursed," Julio said.

Albert also looked unsure. "I don't believe in curses," he said, "but I do believe in bandits. Shouldn't we find out more about these animals first, Wily? I mean, they wore cloaks, right? They could be anything."

"I saw no faces under their hoods," whispered Maria. "I believe they were zombies."

"Curses, zombies, lost treasure!" exclaimed Wily. "It's just a bunch of criminals trying to find some stolen gold."

"We should contact PSSST and get help," said Albert, folding his arms.

Wily sighed. "OK," he said. "You get back on the motorbike. Find PSSST. But don't tell them that Maxwell Mirage is probably in New York. We need more evidence first."

"Take my map," said Albert, folding it up. "You won't get any reception on your phone out there."

Wily smiled and took the map.

"And take this, too," Albert said, handing Wily an umbrella.

"It's OK, I've got a jacket," said Wily.

"This is a rainforest," said Albert. "When it rains, it really rains. And the umbrella is made of reinforced tungsten. So it's bulletproof, bombproof, everything proof. But – here's the best thing – it's also as light as a feather." He pressed a button on the end and the umbrella collapsed down to a small black tube.

"That's pretty cool," said Wily. "Thanks, Albert."

He put the map and the umbrella in his jacket pocket.

The guinea pigs stepped forwards and each shook Wily's hand.

"Goodbye, señor," Julio said, "I will miss you when you are dead."

"Thanks, Julio."

Wily smiled at them all and headed off alone.

✳ ✳ ✳

The ferns led Wily further and further out of the town, and deeper and deeper into the jungle. Every now and then there would be a gap in the ferns and Wily would be lost for a moment, but then he'd spot another and pick up the trail again.

Wily began to climb a hill. There was a strange track mark in the mud in front of him. Not quite a footprint, more like a series of tiny slashes.

Did bandits leave this trail, Wily thought, *and if so, what kind of animal are they?*

Wily considered what he knew about his enemy. They wore cloaks to hide their identities. They were bigger than guinea pigs. Their chosen weapon was a poison arrow. What could they be? If he was going to get

Simon back, Wily would need to work out who the bandits were – and how to beat them.

The ferns eventually stopped at a cave. Wily peered inside. He couldn't see anything, so he sniffed instead. There were no animal scents – just a very slight hint of burnt wood. He turned on his phone torch and edged inside.

In the centre of the cave, Wily found the remnants of a campfire. He inspected a couple of the charred sticks and guessed that the fire was around two months old. The timescales matched – Julio had said the bandits raided Pebas two months ago.

Wily shone his torch around the rest of the cave. Nothing else had been left behind, but something in the far corner caught his eye. A mark on the wall. He moved closer and saw that it was a message, written in tiny letters with the tip of a burnt stick:

THE GROUND DROPS AWAY SOON,
BUT DON'T JUMP TILL NOON.

What did *that* mean?

Wily was reminded of the Case of the Fishy Philosopher, where he'd had to solve fifty riddles in fifty minutes to stop a bomb going off. But those riddles had been easy compared to this one.

Wily sat down and glanced around the cave.

This will be a pretty good shelter for the night, he thought.

He created a spark by rubbing two of the sticks together and pretty soon the campfire was blazing again.

As the cave grew warmer and cosier, Wily drifted off to sleep.

Soon he was dreaming. He saw giant

animals wearing cloaks diving into huge piles of gold. He dreamed of being caught in a huge spider's web while a goat dressed as a sheep fired at him with poison arrows.

When he woke up with a start, the fire was out and light was shining in from the cave entrance. It was morning.

Wily stepped outside and looked for the trail of ferns. But there was a problem. The trail of ferns led into the cave, but that's where it ended. Did that mean the treasure was in the cave? Wily checked the walls again, but there were no holes, no gaps, no secret passages.

He came back to the riddle: *The ground drops away soon, but don't jump till noon.*

Was that a clue for the treasure trail? It was time to explore.

Wily got out his sky sticks and shot one into a nearby tree. He pulled himself up and

swung across into a higher tree
so he could have a proper look
around.

The cave was on the side of a hill.
At the bottom, Wily could just about make
out the roofs of Pebas. At the top, he couldn't
see anything. The trees just vanished.

Wily swung his way up the hillside and
then, when he got to the last tree, he stopped
just in time. The ground fell away and Wily
found himself staring into a
deep ravine. He leaned
carefully over the edge
of the canyon.

The ravine was hundreds of metres deep and hundreds of metres wide.

How am I going to get across? he thought to himself. *Do I even need to get across?*

The words of the message echoed again: *The ground drops away soon...*

That suggested he was on the right trail.

But don't jump till noon.

That was crazy. Nobody could jump across a huge canyon.

Wily looked at his sky sticks. Albert had said they could reach to about two-hundred metres. He looked over at the other side.

"Worth a try," he said out loud.

He aimed at a tiny shape – it looked like a boulder of some kind – and fired. The ribbon shot forwards, traced an arc through the air and then dropped into the abyss. It hadn't even got halfway across. He needed another plan.

Glancing up and down his side of the canyon, Wily looked for signs of bridges or walkways. He couldn't see any, but he did spot a small group of opossums looking at the other side of the ravine and then looking up at the sun and then looking down into the ravine. What were they doing?

A few minutes later, they were joined by a family of porcupines. They all glanced at the sun and then down into the ravine.

Wily too looked up at the sun: it was right in the middle of the sky. Almost noon.

He wanted to call out to the other animals and ask them what they were doing. But just as he was about to speak, they all stepped forwards and jumped off the edge of the canyon.

Wily had a split second to think.

These animals knew something he didn't.

They couldn't be jumping to their deaths.
He ran forwards and jumped into the ravine.

As he fell, he pulled out his sky sticks. If
he fell by more than two-hundred metres,
he wouldn't be able to fire a ribbon and pull
himself out. He was plummeting like a stone,
twenty metres, forty metres, sixty metres. Had
he just made a huge mistake?

Another second flashed by.

He must have fallen over a hundred metres. It was time to shoot a sky stick before it was too late. As his thumb hovered on the button, he felt a rush of wind underneath him.

The rush of wind became a hot blast. Then a vast gale of fizzing air catapulted him back up. He heard shrieks of laughter in the distance as the porcupines and opossums were sent flying up into the sky, too.

Wily looked down below him and saw steam everywhere. There were geysers and hot springs spouting up from the bottom of the canyon! He'd heard about such things, but never seen anything like it.

Wily glanced across and saw that the porcupines and opossums were riding on the gusts of steam, propelling themselves forwards. Wily did the same, flinging himself from one vent to the next.

Within a couple of minutes, he was nearly at the other side.

Then he felt the air underneath him start to subside. He looked up and saw that the opossums and porcupines were on the other side already. They spotted him and made beckoning gestures, urging him to hurry up.

Oh no, Wily thought. *The geysers only spout for a few minutes.*

As Wily began to fall, he aimed his sky sticks at the far side of the canyon and released them. One missed, but the other went taut.

The geysers had stopped now, and Wily was hanging from the sky stick, swinging over the deadly drop beneath him.

Then he felt one end of his sky stick being tugged. When he got to the top of the canyon, he saw that two of the porcupines were holding the other end of the ribbon.

"Thanks," said Wily. "You helped me out of a hole."

The porcupines smiled. "Don't believe everything you hear about porcupines," one said. "Some of us are friendly."

Wily looked confused. "I haven't heard anything about porcupines…"

But the porcupines had curled up into balls and rolled off, leaving a few needles behind.

LOST IN THE JUNGLE

Wily took his bearings. He was on the edge of a ravine in the middle of the Amazon jungle with no idea which way to go next. He had been following a trail of ferns in the hope of finding either a lost treasure trove, a troupe of bandits, Simon Sheep or all three. But now there were no more clues. Which way was Tunza-Dosh?

He looked around for markings or signs or secret entrances. There was nothing. Just trees and puddles and spiders' webs and anthills. He looked for paw prints, he sniffed the air for a scent of sheep. He was getting nowhere. Perhaps it was time to turn back. But he couldn't go back across the ravine till noon the following day when the geysers started spouting again.

Wily sat down on a rock and sighed. This was a much trickier case than he'd expected. He heard a fluttering overhead and glanced up idly – there, suspended in a spider's web, was a piece of paper.

Quick as a flash, Wily shinned up the tree trunk and grabbed it. It was yellow and slightly soggy, but the message was still readable. It was written in the same ink as the clue about following the ferns.

It was puzzling. Wily's first thought was to call Albert. He checked his phone, but there was no signal. Albert had warned him that would happen.

Then he remembered that Albert had given him a map of the jungle. He pulled it out and tried to work out where he was. He found the canyon and traced it along the centre of the map. Then he looked at his phone again – it had a compass on it – and figured out his exact location. He seemed to be several miles away from any village or town. So where was this note telling him to go?

Wily looked again at the symbols on the note. The first one seemed to be pointing west. "Go west to…" Rain? Arrows of rain? Was someone going to shoot a poison arrow at him again? And did he have to jump off *another* ravine?

The second row of symbols didn't make much sense either. Was that a hand? And a picture of someone crying and someone talking.

Wily folded up the note. He decided to head west and inspect anything on the route that looked like a bow and arrow or a giant hand.

He began to fight his way through the undergrowth, squeezing under branches and hopping over roots. He thought about using his sky sticks to move faster, but he didn't want to miss the next clue.

Then it started to rain. Hard.

There was a picture of rain on the note,

but surely that was a coincidence. Unless there was always rain in this part of the jungle?

Do I have to pass through the rain and find … some arrows … pointing somewhere…? he thought to himself.

The rain was now coming down in buckets. It was soaking his coat and dripping off his bushy tail. Wily took out his umbrella and put it up. But although this kept him dry, it didn't stop the earth underneath his feet getting softer and softer.

A few seconds later, the ground gave way and Wily found himself slithering downhill in a river of mud. He fumbled for his sky sticks, but he was moving too fast. He felt more earth giving way underneath him. He tried to grab something – anything – with his right paw, but everything was moving. In the end he just gave up and lay back, letting himself be carried through the trees on a thundering torrent of earth and water.

As he was being swept along and rolled around, his mind was turning, too. The pictures in the notes became words.

Go West. To. Rain. Bow. Falls.

Wily remembered the map. There was a huge waterfall on its western edge – could that be Rainbow Falls? The only problem was, the landslide was taking him in the opposite direction.

Albert had said the umbrella was extremely strong. Wily flipped it upside down and jumped inside. He stuck his left leg out behind him like a rudder on a boat, and steered the umbrella left and right, looking for a way out of the muddy stream.

Then he saw his chance. A huge tree was teetering on the edge of the landslide. Wily steered towards it and hooked the umbrella handle on to one of its branches. The branch started to bend back, but Wily didn't let go. He saw a rock tumbling past and grabbed it with his feet. He tucked a bigger rock under his spare arm. The branch bent back even further.

When it couldn't bend back any more, Wily let go of the rocks. The branch whipped forwards, flinging him into the sky at great speed. He hurtled across the landslide, over a mountain and through a strip of forest. Then he started to fall.

Wily still had the umbrella in his hand and he held it straight up. Albert had said that it was light as well as strong. The air rushed under it, turning the umbrella into a mini parachute.

"Bravo, Albert," Wily muttered. "Another splendid gadget."

He finally landed in the middle of a wide lake. In front of him was a beautiful waterfall that created multi-coloured spray as it hit the water below. Rainbow Falls.

Wily tucked his umbrella back in his pocket and swam towards the waterfall, then he clambered on to the rocks beside it. The spray tickled his fur as he sat and thought about the images on the note again.

OK, so this was Rainbow Falls. He searched for a rock that looked like a hand or a face. Nothing. He looked for a tunnel or a cave or anywhere that might be hiding the treasure. Nothing. There was no way forwards, this was the end of the trail.

He tried to decode the rest of the symbols on the note.

Hand. Cry. Speaking.

Some letters had been crossed out and swapped in.

And? Kry? Weaking?

And? Weep? Talking?

And Keep Walking!

Go west to Rainbow Falls and keep walking!

Wily looked directly into the waterfall. He could see a dark shape – very faintly – behind the fizzing white curtain of water. He took a deep breath and walked forwards. The water pounded his body and almost knocked him sideways. He put up his umbrella and kept going. The water thundered down on top of him, shaking the handle of the umbrella, but Wily clung on.

A moment later, he stepped out on the
other side. The dark shape he had seen
through the waterfall turned out to be Julius
Hound and Sybil Squirrel.

"OK, Fox," barked Hound. "Start talking."

OPEN SESAME

"Julius!" exclaimed Wily. "What are you doing here?"

Behind the waterfall was a kind of grotto. In one corner, there were three rectangles of rock that looked like doors.

"We're on the trail of a con artist," said Julius.

"Maxwell Mirage. I know," said Wily. "But what's he got to do with the trail to Tunza-Dosh?"

"What trail? And how do you know about Mirage?" Julius said with a scowl.

Sybil jumped in hastily. "We've got Maxwell's old phone, Wily. This morning somebody called it from this exact location."

"Hmm," said Wily. "That confirms my suspicions. Maxwell and the bandits were working together."

"Bandits?" Julius stammered. "Suppose you tell us what's going on."

Wily sighed. "If I help you with your case, will you help me with mine?"

"No," said Julius.

"Yes," said Sybil.

"I'll take that as a yes," said Wily. He told Julius and Sybil about his quest to find Simon, but he didn't say anything about Sally Sheep or how Maxwell had taken on Simon's identity in New York. "If you help me get Simon back from the bandits, I'll tell you where Maxwell is now," Wily concluded.

"Hmm," Julius growled.

"But how can we help?" asked Sybil. "We got the call to Maxwell's phone this morning. It's likely the bandits were here earlier today and then left the area. Taking Simon with them."

"I'm not so sure," said Wily. "They left Pebas two months ago. You said they called Maxwell's phone today, so they're clearly not in a hurry. I reckon they might still be here." He gestured at the three doors in the cave wall. "And I'm guessing one of these leads to the treasure."

Julius frowned. "Let's just blow them all open," he said. "I'll call the explosives team."

"Then the cave will collapse, crushing the treasure, the bandits and Simon," said Wily. "Otherwise – genius."

Julius snarled at Wily.

Wily frowned back.

Sybil rolled her eyes. "Let's look for clues."

They inspected the doors, the ground and the grotto walls.

"Got one!" said Wily, picking up a small pebble tucked into a crevice. It had a piece of paper wrapped round it. The paper read:

ALL THAT GLITTERS IS NOT GOLD.
THERE'S A CATCH IN TALES OF OLD.

"That must refer to the doors," said Sybil. "Look, there's a crack of light coming from under

95

these two. Gold light here. Silver light here."

Wily crouched down and could see flickering light under the two doors nearest to him.

"Well, the gold one will have the treasure in," said Julius, walking towards it. "Let's try that one." He pushed against it. "Won't budge," he huffed.

"The clue says 'All that glitters is NOT gold'," said Wily. He pointed to the door that had nothing but darkness behind it. "I reckon we need to go through this one," he said.

Sybil squatted down next to Wily and nodded. "So what's the second part?"

Wily continued, "There's a catch in tales of old. *A catch … a catch.*"

Julius was still pushing at the door with the golden glow around it.

Wily ran his hand across the surface of the rock, then he ran his fingers underneath the door.

"Here – a catch," he said. He found a small notch in the rock and pressed it. There was a click. "I think we have to lift it, not push it," he said.

Sybil nodded, and together they lifted up the heavy block. When it was about a metre off the ground, Wily whipped out his umbrella and used it to prop up the door.

"Quick, let's get through," he said.

Sybil slipped under, followed by Wily.

"You coming, boss?" asked Sybil.

"That's the wrong door!" Julius called out. "This is the right one!"

At that moment, Wily's umbrella snapped and the heavy door fell back down with a *whoomph*, leaving Wily and Sybil alone in the pitch black.

They both pulled out their phones and turned on their torches. They were in a long dark tunnel.

"How are we going to fight off a cave full of bandits?" Sybil whispered.

"I was hoping to use this," said Wily, picking up the snapped umbrella. He pulled out his sky sticks. "Or these."

He pushed the buttons on the sticks, but they just made a weird fizzing noise. They hadn't survived the mudslide and the swim in the lake.

"Oh well," said Sybil, "at least I've still got my truncheon."

"That's the spirit," said Wily, with a smile.

They walked slowly down the narrow, cobweb-filled tunnel.

"I'm quite excited about seeing this treasure," said Sybil. "Do you think it's real?"

"Maybe," said Wily. "The clues have been difficult. Somebody wants to hide SOMETHING."

They turned a corner and the tunnel became narrower and darker. More cobwebs hung from the ceiling. Then the floor of the tunnel dropped away suddenly. They had to jump down and climb up again almost immediately. Then the tunnel turned a corner.

Shortly after, they heard an eerie moaning sound. Sybil and Wily glanced at each other, but kept moving until they reached a small dark cave with a strange shape in the corner. The shape appeared to be chained to the floor. It staggered to its feet and threw its arms out wide.

"How splendid!" it exclaimed. "You found me!"

BACK FROM THE DEAD

"Simon…" stammered Wily. "Simon?"

"That's right," said Simon. "I'm so glad my plan worked."

"Plan?" asked Sybil.

"Yes, the treasure trail and all that," said Simon.

Wily looked momentarily confused, then his eyebrows shot up. "Hang on, you mean Tunza-Dosh…"

"Doesn't exist!" exclaimed Simon.

"And the Lost Treasure…?" asked Wily.

"Is ME of course!" said Simon. "Shall I tell

you the whole story?"

"Yes, please," said Wily. "I'm beginning to understand parts of it, but…"

"OK," said Simon. "You're in the cave where the bandits keep their prisoners. Gustavo did a deal with them."

"It turns out Gustavo is actually called Maxwell Mirage," said Wily.

"That double-crossing villain!" Simon said. "He paid the bandits to take me away from Pebas. On the way here, I heard them discussing it. Gustavo, or rather Maxwell, as you call him, gave them a gold ring he stole from me and promised them more money when he got to New York."

"I can tell you *why* he did it," said Wily, "but finish your story first."

"I knew I had only one chance of being rescued," said Simon, "and that was by using the legend of Tunza-Dosh. I knew nobody would come and look for *me*. But I thought they *might* try to find the treasure. So I dropped clues wherever and whenever I could – making them look like part of a treasure trail."

"But how? You'd been kidnapped," said Wily.

"My arms were bound, but I could still move them a bit," said Simon. "I scrawled my first note about 'following the ferns' on a map of the town I had in my pocket. Then I dropped a groundfern seed every few steps. The bandits didn't even notice. Groundfern seeds are the favourite food of the nine-legged tree spider. Did you know that?"

Wily remembered the empty pot of groundfern seeds in Simon's hut.

"I always carry at least one pot on me," Simon continued, "in case I spot a hungry-looking specimen. They're also the fastest-growing fern in the jungle. I knew that if I dropped a seed, a fern would appear in less than two weeks. Hey presto – a trail."

Wily remembered how regularly the ferns had been spaced out.

"Whenever the bandits chatted about their plans, I'd listen in – they didn't know that Pablo had taught me Ulbuti, so I could understand every word," said Simon. "Using whatever I had to hand – scraps of paper, bits of burnt stick – I'd create a clue and put it somewhere on the route. Sometimes I used the tree spiders to help me. Like my clue about the Rainbow Falls – did you find that one?"

Wily nodded.

"Well, I could see a tree-spider web suspended between two trees. When the bandits weren't looking, I threw the paper straight at it. I knew that the spiders would

cover it in their wonderful waterproof silk and keep it safe."

"They did," Wily said with a smile. "And let me guess, when you got to the door of the cave back there, they dumped you right on the floor."

Simon nodded.

"And you scribbled that clue about 'All that glitters' so we'd ignore the gold door," said Wily.

Simon nodded again.

"You know, that clue was pretty hard," said Wily.

"They were ALL hard," said Simon. "Whoever heard of a treasure trail with *easy* clues? I had to make it look realistic. And I was right. Because here you are."

"Well, this is the funny thing..." Wily began.

"What?" asked Simon.

"I wasn't actually hunting for the treasure," said Wily. "I was looking for you."

Now it was Simon's turn to look surprised.

Wily explained how Sally Sheep was searching for him and how Maxwell was planning to trick his grandmother.

"Then we've got to get back to New York at once," said Simon. "Have you got something to break through these chains?"

Sybil pulled out her truncheon and whacked the chains as hard as she could. After a few blows, they broke apart.

They ran back up the tunnel, past the cobwebs.

"Ah, you can see my friends have been busy," said Simon. "I'm afraid I did that, too. I had a few baby spiders in my pockets. I released them as they carried me down here. I needed this tunnel to be as dark and gloomy as possible – so you wouldn't try the gold or the silver doors."

Wily kept moving forwards, but turned to ask,

"So what's down the other two tunnels?"

"The gold tunnel is where the bandits keep their stolen treasure. It's gold because of the glow from all the coins and rings."

"And the silver one?"

"It's where they keep their stolen weapons," said Simon. "It's silver because of all the swords and shields."

"So there aren't actually any bandits here right now?" asked Wily.

"No, no," said Simon, "the main camp is further up the mountain."

"So how come someone called Maxwell's mobile from here this morning?" asked Sybil.

"That was probably my guard," said Simon. "No doubt he was ringing Maxwell to ask him where their money was."

"I see," said Sybil.

"No," Simon continued, "the only reason

any bandit would come here now is if anyone
was stupid enough to break into the treasure
cave. Then a deafening alarm would go off..."

Wily and Sybil instantly pictured Julius
throwing himself against the door with the
golden glow. They looked at each other, both
thinking the same thought. A moment later,
an ear-splitting siren echoed through the cave.

Simon looked around in confusion.
"What—? Who—?"

"Come on," said Wily, grabbing
Simon by the arm.

"But every bandit in the area will
come running!" said Simon, shouting
to be heard over the deafening alarm.
"My guard and his brothers only live a few
minutes away."

They raced along the tunnel. When they
came to the place where the tunnel floor

dropped away, they jumped down and then up again.

"Who are the bandits?" shouted Wily, as the alarm continued to echo. "What kind of animal are they?"

"I don't know," Simon shouted back. "They always wear hooded cloaks. They're a bit shorter than you and a bit taller than your squirrel friend."

"How will they attack us?" Sybil asked.

"With blowpipes," said Simon. "They seem to have an endless supply of poison darts."

As Simon said "poison darts", several clues came together in Wily's head. The dart that had nearly killed him in the Sheep residence. The strange tracks covered with slashes on the Tunza-Dosh trail. And the family of porcupines who had helped him across the ravine saying: "Don't believe everything you hear. Some of us are friendly."

At the same moment, they turned a corner and saw a circle of light. It was the entrance to the tunnel – wide open.

The alarm fell silent and a shape appeared, wearing a heavy cloak.

"Duck!" shouted Wily.

A hail of darts flew over their heads. The darts tinkled against the wall and fell to the floor. Wily grabbed one and stared at it. It was a modified porcupine quill.

The shape at the end of the tunnel had removed its cloak and rolled into a ball.

"It's a porcupine," shouted Wily. "Run back the way we came!"

The porcupine thundered after them down the tunnel, needles flying off his back. Behind him were two other porcupines, also transformed into balls of razor-sharp quills.

"Where are we going?"
asked Sybil. "The tunnel's a dead end!"

"Exactly!" said Wily.

They sprinted down the tunnel. The
porcupines were getting closer all the time.
When they reached the ledge before Simon's
cell, they jumped down and hid. Porcupines
flew past over their heads – Wily counted five –
jumping straight from one ledge to the other.

"Those cloaks aren't just for disguise,"
Wily whispered. "I think they're to stop them

hurting each other with their needles."

"So?" Sybil asked.

"So they take their cloaks *off* to roll into balls," said Wily.

"Ah," said Sybil, smiling. "Then they're not protected any more."

Wily nodded.

There was a brief silence. They couldn't hear any more porcupines coming.

"They'll soon realize we're not in there," Simon whispered, pointing towards the cave.

"I know," said Wily. "The sooner the better." He stood up. "Hey!" he shouted. "We're over here!"

"Have you got wool for brains?" Simon murmured.

This time, there was a thundering sound from both sides. More porcupines were rolling down the tunnel behind them as the porcupines who were in Simon's cave were hurtling back.

"Crouch down under this," said Wily. He pulled out his umbrella. The handle was in splinters, but the top part still worked. He put it over them and peeked through a small rip.

Porcupines were flying above them in both directions now. The first two porcupines crashed into each other in mid-air, showering quills everywhere.

"Ow!" they howled and dropped to the floor.

More porcupines flew into each other, with shouts of "Look out!" and "Are you blind?"

Soon the air was full of howling porcupines and the ground was a sea of kicking porcupines. Quills flew everywhere, tinkling against Wily's umbrella.

"I must say, this umbrella is surprisingly strong," said Simon.

"Come on," said Wily. "It's time to find the mole who invented it."

They climbed back up, leaving the porcupines still fighting each other.

One porcupine jumped up and called out, "They're getting away!"

But the bandit behind him snarled, "You just stabbed me in the leg!" and pulled him back into the sea of struggling arms and legs.

Wily, Simon and Sybil were soon out of the tunnel. There they saw Julius flat on his back, pinned to the ground with porcupine needles. They'd been pushed through his shirtsleeves and trouser legs.

"Set me free. Now!" he barked.

"In a minute," said Wily, bending over and grabbing Julius's police radio. "Calling all PSSST agents, calling all PSSST agents."

There was a vague crackling from the police radio and then some high-pitched feedback.

"That means there are other radios very close by," said Sybil, looking confused.

Wily looked through the waterfall and saw a blue outline. He held up his umbrella and dashed to the other side.

In the middle of the lake, he saw Albert in a speedboat, along with twenty PSSST agents.

CAUGHT IN A WEB

Wily was standing outside the Sheep residence in New York. Next to him stood Simon Sheep, Sybil Squirrel and Julius Hound.

"I don't like this, Fox," said Julius, glaring at Wily. "You know *I'm* supposed to give the orders round here."

"But you did," said Wily. "Don't you remember – this whole plan was *your idea*?"

"Was it?" barked Julius. "Hmm. Actually, I suppose it was."

"You dreamed it up while you were pinned

down by the porcupines," said Wily.

"Hmm, yes. I do remember making a plan," said Julius.

"Of course you did," said Wily. "Now, remember *your idea* about the nine-legged tree spiders helping you to block the exits. Because they can spin webs so fast."

"Er, yes…" said Julius. "Remind me about that idea again."

Wily told him how the spiders could help them to catch Maxwell Mirage.

"And remember *your idea* about waiting out here with Sybil until we've flushed Maxwell out," he added.

"Yes," barked Julius. "I definitely remember *that* idea. And then I get my picture in the papers and you scarper."

Wily nodded. "That's it. Another triumph for PSSST."

He winked at Sybil and she grinned back.
Then she grabbed Julius by the arm and
vanished around the side of the mansion.

"OK, Simon," said Wily. "Remember what I said.
You appear when I whistle. I need him to confess."

Simon nodded and ducked behind a bush.
Wily pressed a button marked "record" on
his phone and then knocked at the door
of the Sheep residence. He heard

footsteps and Maxwell Mirage – still
dressed as Simon – opened the door.
"Hello, Maxwell," said Wily.

For a few seconds, Maxwell blinked at Wily.
Then he burst out laughing. "You worked it out!
But you're too late!" he cackled. "Come in."

He led Wily into the house.

As they walked along the corridor, Maxwell
said to Wily, "Aren't you supposed to be dead?"

"Aren't *you* supposed to be dead?" Wily

replied. "Or at least missing in the jungle?"

"Nice comeback," Maxwell replied with a giggle. "Oh, it's such a shame you're still alive. I thought I'd managed to rid the world of your irritating crime-fighting skills. I know the poison dart missed its target, but I thought throwing you off the Empire State Building had worked."

"So it *was* you – both times? I thought you might have had an assistant."

"No, the first time I heard you rummaging in Sally's room – thanks to the bug in the statue's eye. I was only a block away so I managed to run back quickly. The dart was adapted from a porcupine quill – borrowed from one of my bandit friends."

"I guessed that bit," said Wily. "I thought you might have had help throwing me off the balcony though."

"I realized I'd made a big mistake at the Millionaire's Ball," said Maxwell. "I ate peanuts when I was supposed to be allergic to them. I was terrified of being found out and I needed to get rid of you. So over you went."

Before they entered the drawing room, Maxwell said, "Now, if you'll excuse me, I have to be Simon again. As you'll see, my, ahem 'grandmother' is just signing a document, giving everything she owns to me. There's no point telling her who I really am because she won't believe you."

Wily saw an extremely old sheep leaning over a desk, squinting at a large sheet of paper.

He also saw Sally sitting in an armchair flicking through a magazine. She looked up and her eyes met Wily's. Wily winked at her and put a finger to his lips. Sally nodded.

"I can't make head nor tail of this, Simon,"

said Sheila Sheep. "Why don't you just sign it for me?"

"I can't, grandmother, dear," replied Maxwell. "It has to be you, I'm afraid."

"Perhaps my lawyer can help," said Wily, putting two fingers in his mouth and whistling. "I asked him to join us."

"Oh, did you?" said Maxwell, raising an eyebrow. "And how's he going to join us if I don't let him in?"

"Because I have my own key," said a voice behind them.

Simon Sheep stood in the doorway.

"Simon!" exclaimed Sally, running across to her brother and embracing him.

Sheila Sheep held up her pince-nez glasses to her face. She looked at Simon and Maxwell and Simon again.

"I must be losing my mind," she whispered.

"Grandmother," said Sally, "*this* is Simon. *He's* an impostor!" She pointed a finger at Maxwell.

"I understand why you're confused, Mrs Sheep," said Wily. "This is Maxwell Mirage, one of the world's best con artists. His disguise even fooled PSSST. And my face-mapping software. He spent a month in the jungle with the real Simon studying his every movement and gesture. He even stole Simon's wool to make his disguise foolproof."

"It didn't fool me!" spluttered Sally.

Maxwell was standing very still, looking at Sheila and then Wily.

Sheila was muttering to herself and rubbing her eyes.

"Nice to see you again, Gustavo, or Maxwell, or whoever you are," said Simon, striding across the room and holding out his hand.

"I-I ... don't know what you're talking about," Maxwell stammered.

"You know, the thing that really hurts," said Simon, "is not the fact that you paid the bandits to kidnap me. Or the fact you manipulated my grandmother. It's that ... I really thought you *cared* about the spiders."

"Grandmother," said Maxwell, "it's me – Simon... This is all some plot to steal your money—"

"Money? What money?" Sheila Sheep said

wonderingly. "I don't have any money, dear."

"What?" said Maxwell.

There was a sudden silence in the room.

"I'm afraid it's all spent," said Sheila. "I've got nothing to leave you but debts."

Maxwell blinked.

"Honestly, it's true," Sheila went on. "I had a long phone call with the bank manager only yesterday. He's going to cancel your credit card. And Sally's. I don't know what we'll do."

Maxwell stared into space for a second more. Then he sprinted out of the room.

Wily ran after him, pulling out his phone. "Heading for the front door," he said.

"Covered," said Julius's voice.

Maxwell opened the front door and saw a giant spider's web blocking the exit.

He turned and ran towards the study, opening the window.

"Heading for the side window," said Wily.

"Covered," said Sybil's voice.

Maxwell opened the window and saw another spider's web.

He tried a few more doors before running upstairs, shoving Wily to one side and leaping off the balcony in the master bedroom.

Wily followed him and looked down into the garden, where Maxwell was tangled up in a giant spider's web. Julius and Sybil were standing either side of it, taking photos and jotting down details in their notebooks. Maxwell's disguise had slipped off – he was now unmistakably a goat.

Sybil looked up at Wily. "Solving crime in record time?" she called up to him.

Wily smiled and nodded. He went back downstairs to the drawing room. Sally, Simon and Sheila were all hugging each other.

"Thank you, Mr Fox," said Sally.

"I can't believe that villain had me fooled," said Sheila. "It's probably time I got new glasses. I've had these since 1963."

"I know I need to pay you," Sally told Wily, "but my grandmother was telling the truth. She just showed us a letter from the bank. She's got millions of dollars of debt. We'll have to sell the house."

"I may end up moving back into a cave," Simon said glumly. "To think I dreamed of coming back to New York and setting up a tree-spider sanctuary, where my little friends could spin their amazing webs forever."

"Don't worry about paying me right away," said Wily. "And don't give up on your dreams just yet."

He held up a shimmering diamond.

"Wow," said Sally. "Where did you get that?"

"The Peruvian government had been trying to catch those bandits for years," Wily said. "They were offering a large reward for any information about the gang's whereabouts. Simon's clever treasure trail led me right to their hideout."

Wily handed the diamond to Simon. "This is your reward," he said.

Simon and Sally looked staggered.

"We don't have to sell the house," whispered Sally.

"I can open my sanctuary," stammered Simon.

"You marvellous fox!" gasped Sheila, giving Wily a hug. "I wish we could clone you!"

But at the word "clone", Sally shuddered. "No more doubles, Grandma," she said.

"Sally's right," said Wily with a smile. "I'm afraid that there is now – and there will always be – only ONE Wily Fox."